588

W9-BGX-695

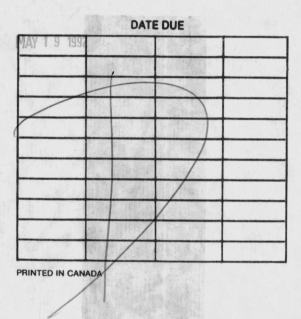

DATE DUE

MAY 1 9 1994

PRINTED IN CANADA

UGLY BIRD

STORY *BY* RUSSELL HOBAN
PICTURES *BY* LILLIAN HOBAN

THE MACMILLAN COMPANY
COLLIER-MACMILLAN LIMITED, LONDON

The Macmillan Company
Collier-Macmillan Canada, Ltd., Toronto, Ontario

Library of Congress catalog card number: 69-11301

Printed in the United States of America

First Printing

For every child who has
heard the world say Yah yah

Once there was a very ugly bird baby,
and his mama loved him.
But all the other birds said, "My goodness,
what a very ugly bird baby that is!"
"Never mind," said Mama to her baby
as she petted him. "They just don't know."

"Don't know what?" said the ugly bird baby.
"Don't know who you are
and what you are," said Mama.
"Who am I and what am I?" said Baby.
"When it's flying time we'll both find out,"
said Mama. "Eat your worm and grow."
Baby ate his worm and grew.

He ate more worms and grew more every day,
and one day Mama said, "It's flying time."
She pushed him off the branch that he
was standing on, and Ugly Bird
fell down until he flapped his wings
and saw that he was falling up.
"Oho!" said Ugly Bird. "I'm flying."
"That's a beginning," said Mama.
"Be home in time for dinner."

So Ugly Bird flew off,
and all the other birds flew after him
and they said, "Yah yah, Ugly Bird."
"Better not make fun of me," he said.
"You will be sorry."
But all the other birds said,
"Yah yah," just the same.

So Ugly Bird put on his stone suit.
Then he went to a boy and he said,
"Put me in your slingshot, please,
and shoot me at those other birds."
The boy shot Ugly Bird
out of his slingshot,
and when he hit the other birds
they all said,
"Wow! What a hard bird!"

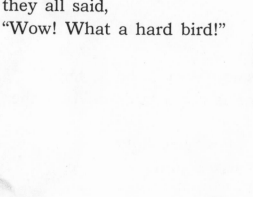

One bird said, "Why is he so hard?"
"Because he is not a bird," said another.
"He is a stone."
The second bird was right.
Ugly Bird was a stone.

He was a very handsome stone,
and when he landed on the ground
a lady stone said, "Hello, Handsome."
"Hello," said Handsome Stone,
but he had to say goodbye because
he was rolling down the hill
to Frog's house by the pond.

"Here I am," he said when he arrived.
"Very good," said Frog.
"You are just in time
for a game of leapstone and skipfrog."
Frog leaped over Handsome Stone first.

Then Handsome Stone skipped over Frog,
and Handsome Stone said,
"On my next turn
I will skip across the pond."
When his turn came he skipped
across the pond in five skips.

But it was a six-skip pond,
and so he sank to the bottom.
"If I have to be wet
I will take off my stone suit,"
said Handsome Stone.
That is what he did,

because he was a shiny fish.
Shiny Fish swam away, smiling to himself
and singing happy fish songs.
He swam until he came to a worm.
"Good morning," said Shiny Fish.
"Good morning," said the worm.
"What time is it?"

"Lunchtime," said Shiny Fish,
and he swallowed the worm.
"Ho ho ho," said the worm
as he was swallowed.
"Now there are two of us on this hook."
The worm was right.
Shiny Fish was hooked.

The hook was on a line, and the line
began to pull him out of the water.
"If this is what happens to fish,
then I will change my clothes,"
said Shiny Fish.

He took off his fish pants
and his fish shirt,
and then he was in his understone,

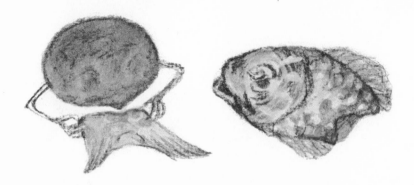

because he was a little pebble.
Little Pebble fell back
into the water with a splash,
and hit a sleeping snapping turtle.
"Good aftersnap," said the turtle,
and he opened his mouth wide.

When the turtle closed his mouth
Little Pebble was inside him.
"Ha ha ha," laughed the turtle.

He thought he had swallowed
something good, and he began
to sing a ha ha ha song.

Little Pebble was in the turtle's stomach,
listening, and he said,
"When you sing ha ha ha
it makes me dance the chachacha."

So he danced in the turtle's stomach.
"I thought that I had swallowed
something good,"
said the turtle, "but I have a feeling
in my stomach that is like
a pebble doing the chachacha."

"That is what I am doing,"
said Little Pebble.
"Maybe from now on you will look
before you say, 'Good aftersnap.'"
"I will do that from now on,"
said the turtle,
"but what should I do right now?"

"You should let me off at my stop,
which is next," said Little Pebble.
So the turtle stopped at the next stop,
which was a log.

Then Little Pebble got out
and took off his understone,
because he was wearing
a buzzing bee outfit under it.
Buzzing Bee buzzed away
from the pond.

He buzzed here and there
among the flowers
until he had a little honey.
Buzzing Bee took a honeycomb
and combed the honey.
He took a honeybrush and brushed the honey.

Then the honey was very pretty,
so Buzzing Bee said, "Will you be my honey?"
"Yes," said Honey.
"Very good," said Buzzing Bee.
"I will visit you again sometime."

Buzzing Bee put on his understone
and he was Little Pebble.

Little Pebble rolled to the pond
and put on his fish pants

and his fish shirt.
Then he was Shiny Fish.

Shiny Fish swam
to the other side of the pond.
He put on his stone suit,
and he was Handsome Stone.

Handsome Stone rolled until he came
to a good place to take off his stone suit,
and he was Ugly Bird again.

Ugly Bird flew home and ate his dinner.
Then he said to his mama, "Ho ho ho."
"Ho ho ho what?" said Mama.

"I know who I am and what I am,"
said Ugly Bird.
"Some of who is handsome
and some is shiny and some is
little and some is buzzing.

Some of what is stone and some is fish
and some is pebble and some is bee."
"Did you say some of who is handsome?"
said his mama.

"Yes," said Ugly Bird.
"I knew it all along," said Mama.
"Now it's time for bed."